MW01094777

YOU HAVE A PET WHAT?!

BEARDED DRAGON

Cristie Reed

Educational Media
rourkeeducationalmedia.com

Before Reading:

Building Academic Vocabulary and Background Knowledge

Before reading a book, it is important to tap into what your child or students already know about the topic. This will help them develop their vocabulary, increase their reading comprehension, and make connections across the curriculum.

1. *Look at the cover of the book. What will this book be about?*
2. *What do you already know about the topic?*
3. *Let's study the Table of Contents. What will you learn about in the book's chapters?*
4. *What would you like to learn about this topic? Do you think you might learn about it from this book? Why or why not?*
5. *Use a reading journal to write about your knowledge of this topic. Record what you already know about the topic and what you hope to learn about the topic.*
6. *Read the book.*
7. *In your reading journal, record what you learned about the topic and your response to the book.*
8. *After reading the book complete the activities below.*

Content Area Vocabulary
Read the list. What do these words mean?

basking
captive
dominance
environment
hatchlings
hydration
mating
nutritional
omnivores
rivalry
submission
temperament

After Reading:

Comprehension and Extension Activity

After reading the book, work on the following questions with your child or students in order to check their level of reading comprehension and content mastery.

1. *What should you ask a breeder before purchasing a bearded dragon? (Summarize)*
2. *What are the environmental requirements for the bearded dragon? (Asking questions)*
3. *What are the most important things to consider when deciding if a pet is right for your family? (Text-to-self connection)*
4. *Why do you think Australia has strict laws to protect bearded dragons in the wild? (Infer)*
5. *How are some bearded dragon behaviors similar to some human behaviors? (Asking questions)*

Extension Activity

What would it cost to become a bearded dragon pet owner? Research the cost of a bearded dragon, a proper enclosure, lighting, pet supplies, veterinary care, and food. Interview a local veterinarian, contact a pet store, and use reliable Internet resources to conduct your research. Create a brochure to share with your classmates, teachers, or parents.

Table of Contents

Dragons: Not Just for Fairy Tales

Imagine having a dragon as a best friend. This dragon can crawl up your arm and perch on your shoulder. No worries about breathing fire. This dragon is tame, curious, and funny.

FUN FACT
Bearded dragons are commonly called beardies.

Bearded dragons are reptiles. Spiny scales run down both sides of their head, throat, and bodies. These soft spines resemble the whiskers of a human and make them look like they have beards.

Their size, playful personality, and good **temperament** make bearded dragons one of the most popular reptiles to keep as pets.

Bearded Dragons: Head to Toe

Bearded dragons have a flattened body and triangular-shaped head with ear holes on each side. Rows of teeth run along the top and bottom of their wide mouth. Their long tail equals their body length. Strong legs make them nimble climbers.

FUN FACT
In the wild, bearded dragons often run on two legs instead of four when they're trying to escape a predator.

ear holes

beard ❯

sharp claws

Beard: The bearded dragon puffs out its throat when it feels threatened.

Tail: The tail is about half the length of its body. Unlike other lizards, it will not fall off and grow back.

Ear holes: Beardies do not have external ear structures, just holes. They have excellent hearing. They can press their ears against the ground and hear vibrations.

Claws: Long fingers with claws help beardies climb trees and other structures.

▲ *Bearded dragons have feet shaped like human hands. Each toe has a strong claw.*

Baby dragons hatch from eggs. The mother digs a hole in sand and lays 11 to 30 oval-shaped eggs. She covers her eggs and leaves them alone to hatch in the warm sand. About two months later, they emerge.

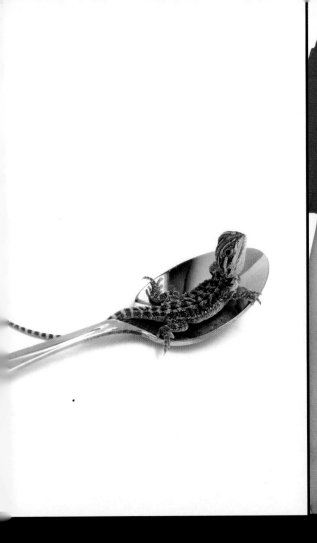

Hatchlings start out two to four inches (5.08 to 10.16 centimeters) long. They reach full size in 12 months. Adults range in size from 12 to 24 inches (30.5 to 60.96 centimeters) and weigh between 12 and 20 ounces (340 to 567 grams). Bearded dragons live up to eight years in the wild. In captivity, they live between 12 and 14 years.

Bearded dragons are typically brown or gray. But many color variations called morphs have been created by breeders. Morphs range in color from red to yellow.

Their skin can be silky smooth or bumpy. While growing, beardies shed their skin every three to four weeks. When full grown, they shed twice per year.

Shedding occurs in patches. Beardies eat less and are less active when shedding.

Land of the Bearded Dragons

Bearded dragons exist naturally only in the desert regions of Australia. They live throughout the continent, but specific types of dragons vary from place to place.

Woodlands, savannahs, and deserts are their natural habitats. They are commonly seen **basking** on rocks or climbing through trees and bushes.

Bearded dragons were first introduced in the United States in the early 1990s. Some experts speculate that a group of Australian bearded dragons were smuggled into the United States illegally.

Today, any bearded dragon in the U.S. was bred and raised in captivity. Reptile owners consider them to be one of the best lizard pets.

TAKE ME HOME!

This reptile enjoys being with humans. Very rarely do they show any aggression. They will sit and relax on a person's body. They enjoy being handled and stroked. They are fairly easy to maintain and don't require walks!

Sit back and watch beardies be themselves. Observe their unique ways of communicating. They make no sound except for some hissing when frightened.

Bearded dragons are typically social. Lizards of similar sizes can live together.

Body movements and color changes indicate their moods. Beardies commonly use head-bobbing to show **dominance**. Arm waving shows **submission**. Their beards flare out and darken when they feel threatened or when **mating**. Color changes occur during **rivalry** and temperature changes.

Behavior	What the Bearded Dragon is Saying
Head-bobbing	"I'm the boss." Or "I want to flirt."
Waving	"I'm friendly."
Color Change	"I'm relaxed." Or "I'm feeling stressed."
Gaping Mouth	"Feed me. I'm hungry!"
Beard Puffing	"Watch out! I'm the boss." Or "I want to flirt."
Beard Puffing, Darkening, and Gaping Mouth	"Watch out! I'm getting angry!"
Body Tilting	"See how big I am?"
Biting	"Don't hurt me!" or "I want to flirt."
Raised Head	"Look at me!"

Baby dragons should be at least six weeks old before they come home with you. Whether you choose a baby or an adult, look for a pet that is plump, alert, and healthy. They should have clean skin and clear eyes.

Beardies can be nervous at first, but they quickly warm up to their humans. When a beardie first comes home, it needs time alone in its new enclosure. Talk to it. Watch to see what it wants to do. Your pet needs to know you are not a threat.

Let your pet get to know you. Gently stroke the beardie along its head and back. You want your bearded dragon to get used to you holding and petting it, but start slowly. Offer it food treats as rewards.

Happy, Healthy Beardies

A healthy dragon is a happy dragon. These **omnivores** have hearty appetites and special **nutritional** requirements. They require a balance of live insects and leafy, green vegetables.

Insects must be raised especially for pet consumption. Offer only clean, fresh vegetables. Feed fresh fruits as a snack. In captivity, their diet needs to be supplemented with vitamins and calcium D3.

Bearded dragons can eat some flowers and flower petals.

Adult dragons need 80 percent leafy greens and 20 percent insects. Feed adults once or twice daily. Baby dragons need 80 percent insects and 20 percent greens. Feed babies several times a day.

▲ *Insects and vegetables should be small enough to fit between the lizard's eyes. Food that is too large could cause choking.*

Foods to Keep Your Bearded Dragon Healthy

Recommended Insects	Recommended Vegetables	Fruit for Occasional Snacks
black soldier fly larvae butterworms crickets Dubia roaches earthworms locusts redworms superworms	artichoke hearts bell peppers bok choy butternut squash cabbage celery collard greens dandelion greens endive kale mustard greens peeled cucumber yellow squash	apples apricots bananas grapes kiwi mangos melon peaches pears plums strawberries

Pet Pointers

Foods to Avoid: Beardies should not eat lettuce, spinach, avocadoes, insects from the wild, or fireflies. Bearded dragons, especially babies, should not consume mealworms.

Dangerous for Dragons: There are many plants and flowers that can be harmful or poisonous for bearded dragons. Check with a reptile specialist to learn more about unsafe foods.

Dragons have special requirements for **hydration**. They take in water through their skin, so they need soaking or misting often. They need a constant supply of fresh water for drinking. Regular baths allow them to soak and drink at the same time.

▼ *Use a soft toothbrush to gently scrub the dragon during bathtime.*

A proper indoor **environment** should mimic their natural habitat. Special reptile cages ensure proper safety, temperature, and lighting.

Beardies need 12 to 14 hours of light during the day and no light at night. Reptiles need both UVA and UVB light rays. Proper lighting promotes digestion and warmth for basking. Temperatures should be 80 to 85 degrees Fahrenheit (26.7 to 29.4 degrees Celsius) during the day and 70 to 74 degrees Fahrenheit (21.1 to 23.3 degrees Celsius) at night.

Like all pets, bearded dragons need regular check-ups from a veterinarian. Expect the vet to examine their eyes, mouth, and skin to see if anything looks wrong. Beardies need yearly checks for signs of internal parasites.

Pet Pointers

Bearded dragons have a cloaca, or vent, for releasing urine and feces. A vet will check this vent to be sure it is not clogged.

Protection for Bearded Dragons

Australia has strict laws to protect bearded dragons. In the 1960s, they banned the sale of wild bearded dragons to the pet industry. Beardies cannot be taken from the wild. In Australia, pet owners need a license to keep a bearded dragon as a pet.

Department of Environment and Primary Industries

Victoria State Government

Private Wildlife Licence Application Form and Guide to Keeping Wildlife for Private Purposes in Victoria

Wildlife Basic Licence
Authorises the holder to possess, keep, breed, buy, sell and dispose of any wildlife (whether alive or dead) listed in Schedules 2 and 7 of the Wildlife Regulations 2013 for non-commercial purposes.

Wildlife Advanced Licence
Authorises the holder to possess, keep, breed, buy, sell and dispose of any wildlife (whether alive or dead) listed in Schedules 2, 3 and 7 of the Wildlife Regulations 2013 for non-commercial purposes.

Wildlife Specimen Licence
Authorises the holder to possess, keep, buy, sell and dispose of prepared or mounted specimens of any dead wildlife for non-commercial purposes.

This form is not valid after 30 June 2015.

1. Your personal details

Mr/Mrs/Ms	First name		Other name/s	Surname

| Date of birth | Sex (M/F) | Concession (Y/N) | To receive a concession on the cost of your licence, you must inclu a photocopy of your pension card with this application. | |

the premises specified in the Licence, unless subject to lawful trade or treatment by a

House/Lot No.

In the United States, bearded dragons must be **captive** bred only. People who breed or sell these animals must have a permit. Bearded dragons should never be released into the wild. This would be cruel to the animal and a threat to the environment.

Things to Think About If You Want a Bearded Dragon

- Male bearded dragons should be housed alone to prevent fighting with other males and breeding with females.
- Bearded dragons live up to 14 years in captivity.
- Pet owners need a fairly large indoor area for the bearded dragon's enclosure.
- Dragons need UVA and UVB light. Their habitat needs to be kept at proper temperatures.
- Equipment and supplies for their indoor habitat can be costly.
- Bearded dragons thrive on a daily routine for feeding, light, hydration, and attention.
- Environmental needs make traveling difficult.
- Bearded dragons can carry a disease called salmonella. Always wash hands before and after handling.

Glossary

basking (BASK-ing): to lie or sit in the sunshine and enjoy it

captive (KAP-tiv): captured and held in a cage

dominance (DOM-uh-nuhns): to show power or control

environment (en-VYE-ruhn-muhnt): your surroundings; all things that influence your life

hatchlings (HACH-lings): recently hatched animals

hydration (hye-DRAY-shun): to supply enough moisture or water

mating (MAT-ing): to join together for breeding

nutritional (noo-TRISH-uh-nuhl): provides substances that the body can use to stay strong and healthy

omnivores (OM-ni-vorz): animals that live on a diet of both plants and animals

rivalry (RYE-vuhl-ree): a competition between two creatures

submission (sub-MISH-uhn): to obey someone or something

temperament (TEM-pur-uh-muhnt): your nature or personality; the way you usually think, act or respond

Index

Show What You Know

1. What are the challenges and benefits of having a bearded dragon for a pet?

2. Describe the proper home environment for a bearded dragon.

3. Explain the important nutritional requirements for bearded dragons.

4. How do bearded dragons communicate with each other?

5. Using the chart and photos on page 10, explain the similarities and differences between each type of bearded dragon.

Websites to Visit

http://a-z-animals.com/animals/bearded-dragon

www.beardeddragonguide.com

www.thebeardeddragon.org

About the Author

Growing up on a small farm in southern Indiana, Cristie Reed was surrounded by an assortment of farm critters including cows, chickens, goats, ducks, cats, dogs, and a pony. After moving to Florida, she got to know anole lizards, a caiman, more dogs and cats, a pet squirrel, and a very special peacock. Cristie is a lifelong literacy teacher. Reading and writing about animals is her favorite hobby. She lives in central Florida with her husband, a miniature schnauzer named Rocky, and a new puppy named Adrienne.

Meet The Author!
www.meetREMauthors.com

www.rourkeeducationalmedia.com

PHOTO CREDITS: Cover: Tbintb; page 1: ©Tbintb; page 1, 14: ©NunyaCarla; page 3: ©GlobalIP; page 4: ©Aurora Photos; page 5: ©Shoretie; page 6-7: ©ericsphotography; page 8, 11: ©bluedog studio; page 9a: ©Rebel_Muse; page 9b: ©Maica; page 10: ©bluedog studio/Shutterstock; page 12: ©Juanmonino; page 12b: ©gaurav_gadani; page 13: ©adogslife; page 15: ©pmcdonald; page 16-17: ©Linda Yolanda; page 18: ©Myrleen Pearson; page 19: ©Stanley45; page 21: ©benzymo9024; page 22: ©Tommy1X; page 23: ©Gina Kelly; page 24: ©Brian Owens; page 25: ©Pavlin Plamenov Petkov; page 26: ©Rommel Canlas; page 27: ©titoOnz; page 28: ©marsipanes; page 29: ©Paul Wood

Edited by: Keli Sipperley
Cover and interior design by: Rhea Magaro-Wallace

Library of Congress PCN Data

Bearded Dragon / Cristie Reed
(You Have a Pet What?!)
ISBN 978-1-68342-180-1 (hard cover)
ISBN 978-1-63432-246-4 (e-Book)
Library of Congress Control Number: 2016956602

Also Available as:

Printed in the United States of America, North Mankato, Minnesota